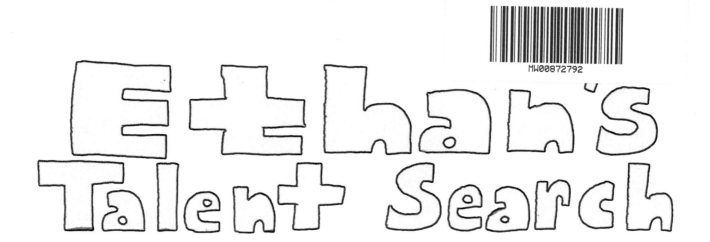

Ethan's Talent Search

By Eric Woodyard & Sharonda Jones
Illustrated by Shelby Baxter

To my granny Onquette "Snoop" Woodyard, Kierra "Ke Ke" Woodyard, Lorraine "LuLu" Norwood, Rashan "Shani" Ramsey, and my great grandparents, John and Liz Burnett, thank you all for being a part of my life. Also, rest in Heaven to my grandparents, Julia Jones and David Johnson. Love y'all.

— *Beater*

Ethan can
stroll.

Ethan
can
throw.

But when it's time to **bowl** with Kadyn,

the **gutter** is where his ball seems to go.

Maybe one day his punches will grow to be as strong, but for now all Ethan can do is admire his big cousin's technique from Hong Kong.

Whenever Ethan comes around he teaches him how to *hit* and *fast-pitch*.

Acting is Nas' *gift.*

He practices his line with Ethan every day as they read through the **script.**

Antoine is good in the **band**.

Ethan is an entirely different story, on the other *hand*.

Amir can rhyme and *flow*. It's evident that he will someday put on a *show*.

He has the skills to make it to the *top*.

But in
Ethan's case,
he's not as
lyrical in
hip-hop.

When Ethan gets home to his mommy and daddy, he cries out of frustration as they encourage him to keep trying badly.

He raises his arms up sadly, asking them to "pick me up!" But both parents aren't going for that crybaby stuff.

"Don't ever give up when you play," Daddy says. "You can't lose as long as you try to get better every day!"

So although
Ethan is *small*

and some of his friends at school are **_much taller_**.

"When it comes to playground hoops at recess,

Ethan turns out to be a real legit *baller.*"

He can *shoot* and *pass*,

but he knows
he has to be
just as good in
class.

Drawing is another one of Ethan's *gifts*,

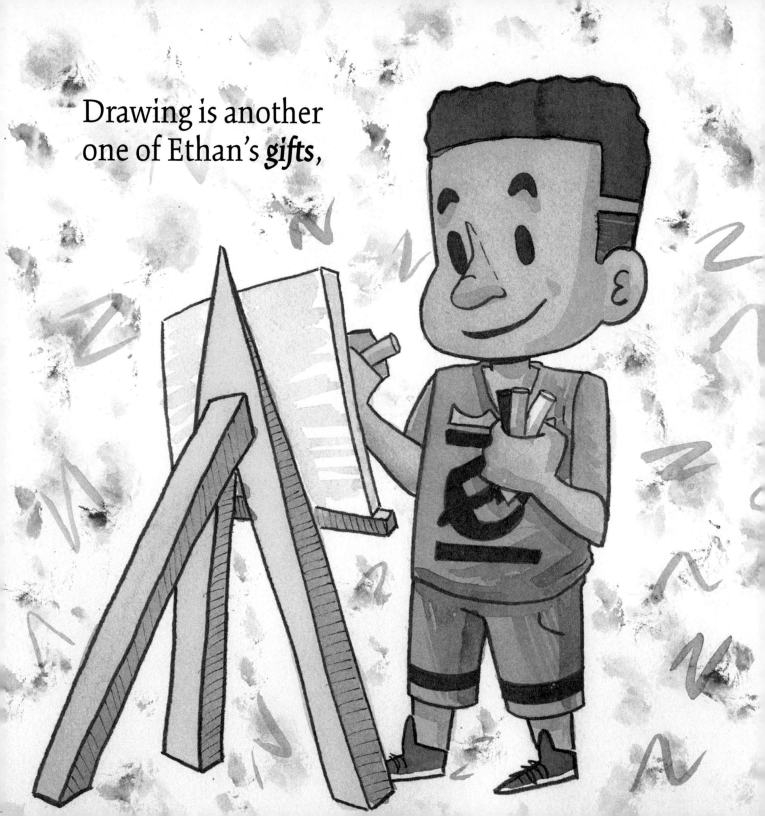

but he wouldn't have known that had he decided to *quit*.

30816212R00018

Made in the USA
San Bernardino, CA
29 March 2019